Friendship Adventures

Three Short Stories

Callie Rae

For those making the world a better place spreading kindness, love and happiness...

Copyright © 2021 Callie Rae

All rights reserved.

ISBN: **978-1-7398174-0-4**

Contents

Rae Rotter Changes the World   1

A Day in Space   14

The Almost Black Christmas   28

"Ha, ha, ha!!" The sound of joyous laughter drifted through the coastal sea air like a cheerful song on a gentle breeze. The Rotter family were on an Easter break - Rae's first trip away from home, being that he had just been born three months previous – 29th January.

Rae was a secure baby whom was deeply adored by his parents, as a first born and only child to be. He had clear, light blue eyes, short, blonde, curly hair and he was always happily gurgling–

not yet knowing that he was going to change the world. His mum, Anna-Marie cradled him in her arms as she listened to the soft hum of the waves.

She had light blue eyes, like her son, and slight brown hair reaching down her back. She loved to wear odd socks with her clothes inside out or the wrong way around, (she liked to be different.) It was her caring but humorous nature that attracted her opposite in Adam, Rae's dad. He marched to a different beat with his short brownish, black hair and chestnut brown eyes. They say "opposites attract" which was definitely the case, they both knew Rae was a special boy, born to live a special kind of life.

No flags were flying on that clear, blue skied morning. Anna-Marie left the content infant as she stepped into the warm waters for a paddle. Removing his shoes and pairing his socks – Adam joined her, just to be with her...

Suddenly, they were swept off their feet and carried away deeper and darker, never to be seen again. Meanwhile an unknown, cloaked individual spotted the infant child, picked him up and they disappeared to a roof top of a London estate. Here Rae bounced down the chimney of ash into the spacious living room of his only living, British relatives, his Grandparents.

As Rae grew, he learned more about who he really was– his love for magic was exceedingly strong, he read about it every day. At ten years old (close to his eleventh birthday) Rae received an unexpected letter in the post.

The bulky envelope had enclosed an invitation and a list of all the things he needed to attend Land High, the transparent bus that explains an orphan's past. "How odd!!" Rae thought as he appeared with his suitcase on an invisiplane. Settling down in his seat marked by a red 'R,' he found a medium sized phoenix feather wand and a snowy white pet owl that he named Sugar.

Rae noticed two seats that were empty, one embroidered with the letter 'R' and the other an 'E.' Empathetically smiling each time a seat was filled, he was accompanied by two others Rose and Eire. Rose was a smart girl with long, bushy hair and grassy green eyes who had learned everything she thought she needed to know for Land High before boarding the plane.

Eire however, was different. He was confident but found learning exhausting. As the final person got to their seat behind Rae, he turned around to see a person who looked like they had just scoffed a lot of chocolate – smirking and sniggering with those around him. During the flight Rae, Rose and Eire found that they had a lot in common – from their experiences, to their personalities, to their passions that they wanted to follow in the future – they agreed to keep in touch. Rae asked who the boy behind was, keeping a good distance away so as to not get hurt from this individual's impolite actions that he had observed. He was right! The response came with an attempted kick, "I'M WONKA! WHO WANTS TO KNOW?" he questioned sarcastically.

Later that day, the invisiplane touched down in Florida, right in front of the transparent double decker bus, Land High. Waiting to escort the anxious orphans that possess magical capabilities on board, was a tender-hearted wizard who looked like a lion, named Puppy. He pounced forward to greet them in a jolly way and they cautiously followed him onto the bus, unsure of what to expect. Inside was a colour-changing, furry sight with owl pictures all over the walls.

Rae, with Sugar perched on his shoulder for company, studied the pictures that showed flashbacks to his childhood. He slowly began to piece the puzzle together of the misery and devastation of his parents' unexpected deaths. Puppy padded over to the tearful young boy, whispering softly the details of what had tragically happened all those years ago. Puppy wrapped his paws around him and led him back to the plane.

On the way home, Rae explained what he now knew to his fellow orphans, until he was rudely interrupted by Wonka returning to his seat, mocking what he had just overheard. "Special boy! Oh yeah, change the world! Good one Rotter!!"

The three amigos stood up together, politely asking that he sat down so that they could take off for home.

Finally he sat down, they explained to him, "Being unkind doesn't get you true friends." Then they invited Wonka to join their friendship circle of happiness and love.

Back home in Britain, they all said their goodbyes and promised to spread kindness and love.

To be the change in the world.

Foxes Way, down South, a long road with three pathways that led to the beach. One muddy, one stony, and the last one with arching trees that created a tunnel of bird song. Along the road there were fifteen large houses of which three stood out; a red one, a green one and an orange one. The residents of these three homes were good friends, nature lovers and good readers who were keen for adventure. Over the road was a big field that the friends loved to play on. There - they let their imaginations run wild. Their favourite game was seeing how many grasshoppers and crickets they could catch in the tall grass stalks.

JJ and Snapper (his midi, green dragon) often caught the most grasshoppers. The eleven-year-old, spikey haired, blue-eyed boy always loved suggesting an adventure, but today he had a different idea, to ask his friends for suggestions as he jumped out of his house with his dragon at his heels. Next door, his friends Roxie and Pickle came out to meet them and said "We have some ideas of what we should do today!" They danced an Irish jig as they headed to the field. Roxie, was a long haired nine-year-old girl, of average height and able to make people laugh.

Sitting in their usual asteroid crater, Roxie hummed her new YouTube song she had just learned about Dwarf Planets with her black and white porcupine pet, named Pickle. Two minutes later JJ, Snapper, Defeat and CDE11 collapsed into the crater which startled Roxie and Pickle. Defeats fly away red hair tickled Roxie's pale cheek and she giggled as she greeted CDE11 (a live, non-melting snowman.) JJ returned their attention to Roxie's earlier comment. "Excuse me. Roxie, you know when you were talking earlier - what were you going to suggest?" Looking excitedly at her friends, she collected together some freshly cut grass and spelt out P. A. C. E. S. "Can you work out the code?" asked Roxie, as JJ and Defeat thought hard to understand. "Paces? Paces?" they puzzled and muttered between each other. Suddenly, Defeat shouted out "SPACE!!" successfully cracking the code. "Well done!" agreed JJ.

"Let's go to outer space" squealed Roxie full of excitement. "We'll need our transport modes to get there!" exclaimed JJ, "I will run and get them from our garages. While I am away, look for a clear spot to take off from!" Off he ran, leaving the others as the sun rose higher in the sky.

By 9 O'clock, Defeat and Roxie had found a long runway, approximately two hundred metres from the crater, that they could generate enough speed along the flat, compact ground to get up into the air. Defeat instructed Snapper, with his wide wing span to hover above them so that JJ would see where they had got to.

Sometime later, JJ appeared on his brand new, long pedal bike, towing Roxie's lightning bolt scooter behind and commanding Defeat's broomstick to go wherever he needed it to. He untied Roxie's scooter when he arrived back with his friends and Defeat caught hold of his broomstick. Roxie took her scooter and put Pickle onto it, while Snapper flew onto the back of JJ's bike. JJ pedalled as Roxie scooted beside him and Defeat ran alongside them with his broomstick carrying CDE11. Faster and faster, they were picking up speed managing to get up, up, up and out into the Milky Way.

When they were floating in the Milky Way, they asked each other what planets they thought they should visit and what they might see there. Roxie said "I think we will see asparagus on Uranus."

"Ketchup bottles on Haumea." suggested Defeat.

"We'll see stingrays swimming in creamy chicken soup on Mars." JJ replied.

CDE11 muttered "Lava rivers on Mercury."

"I think we will see snakes on Jupiter," roared Snapper.

"Witches on Venus." Pickle squeaked.

"And walking fish on the moon." They all chorused together.

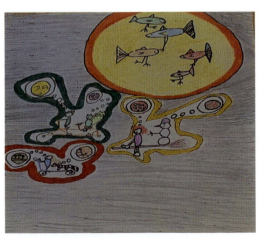

Suddenly they heard a frightening squeal. Pickle had fallen from the back of the scooter and he was heading straight for a **BLACK HOLE**. It was sucking him in. All of a sudden, JJ had an idea. He had a net in his bag that was carrying his lunch. He attached a rope to the net and kept hold of one end, telling Defeat and Roxie to grab hold of the middle. He called out "3, 2, 1!!" and threw the net for Pickle to catch. The net tangled into the spikes of the tumbling porcupine. The friends worked together and managed to pull him back to safety onto the transport mode. They then set off for the planet Haumea. When they got there, Defeat shouted "Yes!! I was right." JJ and Roxie cheered, they had a look around and saw that something was wrong – the ketchup lids were coming loose. They worked quickly, managing to screw each lid back on.

Off they went to Uranus. Roxie cried "Yes!! I was right." JJ found a couple of loose asparagus stems and put them into his bag to take home for dinner. After that, they orbited Mercury and CDE11 muttered "Right again, as always." Floating down to the moon they saw a walking grey tang. At first, they thought there was only one, until they spotted two more. Not wishing to disturb the fish, the friends turned to Venus to see witches flying about on their broomsticks. Pickle gave a squeal of delight when he saw that he too had been right with his idea.

One of the witches saw them and beckoned them over. They had a little tea party and were challenged to catch a snake from the planet Jupiter. The witches told them which colours to avoid and which snakes were safe. "Ha, ha!" Snapper breathed a fire bolt. "Very funny, c'mon let's go! I can catch any kind of snake, poisonous or not!"

It took a little while to get to Jupiter. Snapper reminded the group that he had said earlier that they would see snakes there. They then managed to catch a poisonous snake using the same proceeding as they had done earlier to save Pickle. Letting the snake go, they headed off to Mars.

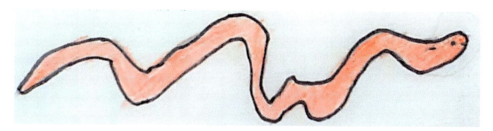

When they finally got there, JJ quietly said "I was right about the chicken soup! But I can't see any stingrays." All of a sudden, Roxie noticed two eyes breaking the surface of the chicken soup. She tapped JJ on his shoulder and pointed to where she had seen the eyes. JJ saw them and was delighted that he had been correct in his view. He took out the camera from his bag, (the one that he had been using to take photos of all the planets that they had visited.) He snapped a few more of Mars and put the camera away for safekeeping, just in time. A meteor shower was heading their way.

Just before it hit them, JJ signalled to his friends that they should go home because it was getting late and they needed to cook their dinner. So they shot off through Earth's atmosphere, landing on the white sandy beach near to where they lived. Walking home through the tunnel of birdsong, they agreed to make a scrapbook about their day in space. They marvelled at how amazing the universe is, with and without gravity – a natural force – but all they really need to survive is each other – FRIENDSHIP.

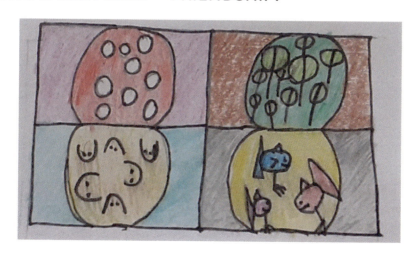

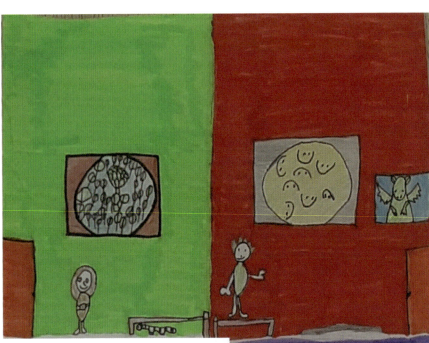

JJ, Defeat, and Roxie met at the asteroid crater to complete their scrapbook and each of them picked their favourite photograph to put on their bedroom wall.

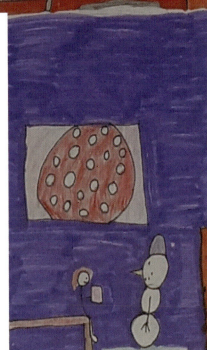

JJ liked the eyes in the chicken soup.

Defeat's favourite photograph was the ketchup lids popping off.

Roxie's best part was seeing the tallest asparagus tree.

They all went to JJ's house for a dinner of tasty asparagus stems freshly harvested that day and to suggest what their next exciting adventure could be.

The Almost

Black
Christmas

Prologue

Once upon a festive season, up at the North-Pole, Santa and his elves were rushing around. All of a sudden, an elf shouted,

"SAAANNNTTTAAAA! The bag of musical toys has vanished!"

The elves gasped and the atmosphere turned tense. Santa raced over, scanned the floor and then the air - a single black feather floated gently to the ground. Santa went forward and picked it up, "The Black Gulls!" said Santa quietly.

"What do we do?" asked an elf, called Frost.

"WE CALL THE CHRISTMAS CARERS!" demanded Santa. "Frost! You go and get them, they're always ready for a dangerous adventure." Santa continued, "Jack! Go, get the snow dogs ready in the yard! But leave Bee and Jake in the kennels to rest because of their conditions. Everybody calm down 'THE CHRISTMAS CARERS' are on their way!"

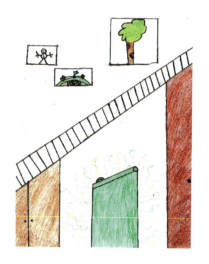

Chapter 1

The Christmas Carers were in their back garden having a ferocious snowball fight. The huge space that surrounded their small on the outside, big on the inside two bed-roomed-house had been covered with a blanket of crisp, white snowflakes overnight. It was lots of fun for the siblings, who all got on together (usually.) There was an enormous amount of space with several wide trunked oak trees for them and their dogs to play among. When unexpectedly their two black and white pointer dogs, Jo and Sandy, started talking like people. The four children shot looks of concern at each other. When their dogs started talking like that, it normally meant that things at the North Pole were in need of some brave, helping hands.

"To the *TIME MACHINE*!" said James. (James was nine years old and had a big imagination.)

"We don't have a time machine. Come here, Jo!" Treasa shouted. (Jo was Treasa's favourite dog.)

"You're right, we don't! We've got something that is better than a time machine. It's a *'Bin there, done that'* machine." yelled Friday with a wink, running towards the house. "I hid it in the old cupboard no-one ever uses and I've been tinkering with it over the past few weeks." (Friday was very good at making things that work.)

"Smashing F!" said Paddy. "Come on everyone! You too Sandy!" he urged approaching the open door. (Paddy was the oldest but didn't tell the others what to do.)

They all ran inside and tiptoed to the unused cupboard under the stairs - and there was the '*GREAT*' machine...

AN OLD, STINKY, GREEN BIN!

"It's wonderful. Well done, Friday." Treasa gasped. She sniffed the foul - smelling air, screwing up her face.

"Let's go! Let's go!" yelled James.

"Shhh James! We don't want Mum to find out." Paddy whisper shouted.

"Don't just stand there! Let's go! Christmas is in two days!" whispered Friday, shimmying the others inside. She shut the lid and pushed the big, orange start button while the others pushed and shoved each other for more space crammed inside the bin, with the dog's tails tickling each of their nostrils.

THEY WERE ON THEIR WAY.

Chapter 2

They landed with a bump in front of Jack and the sled of harnessed snow dogs in the snowy outback.

"Hello. Are you The Christmas Carers?" he asked.

"Yes! What's happened?" enquired Paddy.

"It was the Black Gulls! They stole the musical toys." Jack explained. "They have a dark, cold, damp cave in the tallest mountain. You need to head North-East. Their cave is guarded by a giant stinky YETTY."

"I love the sled dogs." said James. "But two dogs are missing," he pointed out

"I know! One is pregnant and the other is sick. I don't know how this is going to work." Jack cried.

"We can help!" panted Jo "How about it, Sandy?" he asked his companion.

"Ok." barked Sandy wagging her tail joyfully. Jack harnessed them to the sled alongside the other excited hounds.

"Will you come with us?" Treasa asked Jack warily as she thought about how scary the Yetty might be.

"Yes! Let's get going." Jack responded. They zoomed over hills, the dogs jumped over valleys and after many bumps in the uneven terrain, they came to a halt. They had arrived at the mountain cave hidden above the clouds.

"Here we are. Be careful!" Jack instructed. "Make a snowball each and make them big!" he ordered. "Friday, throw your snowball into the middle entrance... NOW!" commanded Jack.

Chapter 3

A giant Yetty emerged, roaring and shaking the loose snow from its dirty coat of matted fur. The sound echoed across the empty, snow-covered plains of the Artic.

"Snowballs at the ready! Aim! Fire!" screamed Jack and four

more tightly compacted snowballs flew through the air directly towards where the Yetty was standing.

Meanwhile, Friday was unharnessing Jo and Sandy from the sled - ready for what she was sure to be – 1, 2, 3, 4 direct hits.

The Yetty toppled over and the seven of them ran into the cave and were faced with a giant maze of ice mirrors reflecting the light from the entrance.

James ran forwards and crashed into an ice mirror.

"Ouch! That hurt. I didn't see that!" he cried clutching his nose. "We need to do something about these mirrors." He groaned.

"Let's smash them," said Treasa with a steely glint of determination in her eyes.

"What with?" questioned Jack frantically looking around the cave entrance.

"With rocks of course!" chorused Jo and Sandy pawing at the floor of the cave.

So, they set about smashing the mirrors. Then Sandy started barking and growling like a steamroller. They all looked up and then they heard the big forbidding squawk of a Black Gull.

"You will never get to the place where we hid the presents, and if you do, we will be waiting for you!"

It laughed a mean cackle and flew away like an illusion.

"How mean!" Paddy exclaimed. "What do we do now?" he questioned with exasperation in his voice.

"Keep smashing the ice." Friday said, with a shrug.

At last all of the ice was demolished and they found themselves faced with a fast-flowing river. A carved, wooden canoe with a sharp ice-breaker attached to bow was awaiting them moored to the icy bank.

"Friday, can you take us along the river in that canoe safely?" barked Sandy sniffing the air for the scent of the gulls' lair.

"Yes. I can. I just need everyone to be careful that it doesn't tip." Friday replied. Cautiously she balanced the weight of them all in the small vessel. She heaved the boat into the flow of water. The ride was very bumpy as they hit a lot of icebergs, but the ice breaker did its job well, so that they didn't end up like the Titanic.

Finally they came to a large meander in the river where a black tributary signalled that the gulls were close by. James spotted the Black Gulls perched on the bag of musical instruments in the middle of a great hall of ice.

"We knew you would come," they sneered. "But it's not very surprizing - you still can't have the instruments." they sniggered.

"I know! We can have a musical competition and the winner keeps them," suggested Jo as the fur along his hackles stood on end. He was poised for a battle, a battle of the bands. His ears pricked up and his head was held high as he snarled, baring his sharp fangs at the scraggly, old birds.

"OK!" The Black Gulls scoffed, gliding over to the new arrivals.

"Pick an instrument! A one, two, three – Go!"

They played for a reindeer judge who had been taken hostage by the gulls some weeks previous. The Gulls felt they were sure to win, loving how their tune was being played. It sounded like a violin bow on a serrated wire.

The Christmas Carers won with a perfectly sounding Jingle Bells, gently played on a xylophone and some handheld bells. But the Black Gulls did not give them the sack...

Chapter 4

All of a sudden Rudolf appeared through a gaping hole in the rocks. The Black Gulls were petrified. With a squawk, they flew away. "Thank you, Rudolf. Let's go back to Santa and tell him that the musical instruments are safe!" Jack cried. They got back to the panicking grotto as quickly as they could. They each thanked Frost for alerting them through the dogs.

"SANTA!" James and Treasa shouted ecstatically as they sprinted towards the red coated figure standing in front of the grotto.

"Yes, it is me!" boomed Santa. "Do you want a hug?" he asked.

"Yes, please!" James and Treasa replied, wrapping their arms around his wide waist.

"Well done, all of you Christmas Carers, elves and Rudolf." cheered Santa. "Now Christmas Carers I think it's time for you to go home." The children agreed that they needed to get home before their mum noticed that the house was deserted.

"Come on then," ushered Friday "Good bye Santa, see you

tomorrow!" he called running back to where they had landed.

They jumped into the *'Bin there, done that'* machine looking forward to getting 'the T-shirt' for Christmas and were gone with a whistle.